HER SUNS AND THEIR DAUGHTERS

DAUGHTERS OF THE UNIVERSE SEEN

by D.C.THOMAS

Her Suns And Their Daughters: DOTUS by D.C.Thomas

Her Suns And Their Daughters: DOTUS by D.C.Thomas

D.C.THOMAS

Copyright © 2020 D.C.Thomas

ISBN: 9798599922087

Her Suns And Their Daughters: DOTUS by D.C.Thomas

Her Suns And Their Daughters: DOTUS by D.C.Thomas

CONTENTS

For mom, and for all the women before us …

Art by D.C.Thomas, 2017

Her Suns And Their Daughters: DOTUS by D.C.Thomas

THE GROUND

Her Suns And Their Daughters: DOTUS by D.C.Thomas

I

Grounded,
Deserted,
In abandoned lands she finds herself,
With worlds behind, of many souls,
Her heart won't cease the work
That got her walking on this Earth.

In the many faces danger built for war,
She found her image in a water drop
Falling from the flask she holds,
Linked to the armor one can't disrobe.

Difficult to say if fight still breathes within
her, 'cause she closed the eyes when she parted
with the soul,
On a stranded planet, with no purpose left,
And barren lands that oddly make her stand.

II

The Silk Road has many routes,
Stretching vastly from North to South,
Through Mountains, plains and
steppes,
Deserts 'n' rivers from East to West,
Sought and walked by many steps.
In such lands of wealthy trades,
A queen in silky cloak awaits,
For a merchant to prevail
In a quest that's splitting maps,
With hidden perils,
Endless gaps,
And groups of men wearing masks.

He fought the beasts into the ground,
Their roars soared to sky
In waves of sound,
Like ripples ruffle water swamps,
Found in soils of clay and sand.

III

The wind today,
The bowls of clay
Keep their ground,
But water cometh
In falling droplets,
The clay is breaking,
And summer endeth.

IV

My head rests on the pillow,
It's morning, it's fall,
I hear people harvesting
What they've sown.

V

Celtic stones adorning hills,
Rumors whispered by the trees,
At night, when she deeply sleeps,
Life takes place in her dreams.

VI

Those sugar fields, yearning for the burning
Sun,
Dancing feet of young girls -
Picking flowers and running,
Flattening the tall summer grass.

VII

There's more than just one hill,
The land is bubbling in front of her eyes,
In the scorching heat of the Sun,
The Earth is dancing and warping in midair,
Too much light,
And none in her soul finding ways.

VIII

This is our room,
Our own world,
Our dream,
Our stage.

IX

Bikes hang in balance ,
At the rear of car,
Spoked wheels remain still,
On par,
And yet, they travel so afar.

X

Fields of sugar cane
Melt in summer's haze,
Warmed by rays of golden Sun,
And rest under stars unsung.

XI

Mine, His and Hers

Sitting by the candle lit fire,
Young daughter of a miner,
Bare hands feasting on father's mails,
Eyes gleaming over ageless tales,
He writes to her
In ink and tears on paper,
Stories never heard before,
Leaving out his daily chores.
The ink he makes out of coal,
The tears he so much wants to hold
Back, from the paper made of rotten cloth,
Thus recording a father's love
For daughter born
In the mid' of night,
Windy and cold,
The mother passed
Giving life
To a child with strong core.

XII

At the gates of the garden
Full of weeds,
Rests a weeping willow
In the mist,
Its roots are drowning
In the water
From the pits,
Where the rains of clouds
Have spilled,
To grow the seeds,
And sink the ships.

XIII

An October's Night

In the air
Filled with the last pollen
Spread by the last warm wind,
Sent from southern lands,
She stares at the vacant benches
In the park,
By the oak trees,
With the ancient riddled barks,
It's night,
A day's end
Filled with cold and fright,
Mud covered boots walk the ground
Covered by the sand
People brought into town,
From afar,
She can't walk anymore,
She's stuck
In this land made by none.

XIV

Her shadow casts
The winter
Over suns
Below the fields
Of this Earth,
Where lives and flowers
Wither and get old.

XV

In her garden
With benches
Made of wood -
Soft and rotten,
She left the goodbyes,
The petty hatred,
And the cries.

XVI

Parting ways appear forepart,
He leans to cross and end the part
He held throughout,
He abstains from choosing path.

XVII

The grass is growing taller
In the arid fields
Around her,
Dried bits falling at the feet,
Of the girl he used to meet.

XVIII

The pens she uses trapped the rainbow,
In a box made of glass,
She lines them up in stacks,
To cover the world in glow.

The light inside of her
Can warm the weakest core -
Of beings living in this world,
Of predators, ghosts and ghouls along.

XIX

She was barefoot on the dew soaked grass,
Then, it started to rain.
She smiled.

XX

Water dripped rock, wrapped in canvas,
Placed by a sunbathing cactus,
On the window's sill, they both rest,
By a sparrow's little nest.

XXI

She leaves behind
Letters tied,
With strings made of grass,
Right outside, by empty glass.

XXII

This tree doesn't need your blood,
To grow its roots
In this poor mud
You brought in
On your boots -
Go back out
And wash your hands,
Ask for forgiveness
And say yes
To a life of pardon,
Scatter seeds in the wind,
Feed the birds,
The ground,
To nature
Remain bound,
Swallow the pride
That makes you hate the man.

XXIII

Should I fall asleep here?
My ankles hurt,
My waist is burning,
Should I lay here?
The clouds want to cry a rain,
My eyes to pray,
The grass is thirsty,
The mold on this fence is so close to me,
I don't want to rest here;
What should we do when life is giving in?
I wish to build a forest in my lungs,
With a clearing,
The meadows seem like a beautiful
dream, I will not rest here,
I will stand and travel,
We will meet, exchange honeyed words,
In another time,
We won't mourn anymore,
Nor shelter pride in our cores.

XXIV

All the bulbs of disbelief
Are rotten -
Feeding seeds - fallen
On the ground last autumn,
The fingerprints, I left on the gardening tools,
Have been covered by the soot
Of all the fires we started.
I wish to sleep now,
And awake my soul in a new era,
During sunny days, filled with light -
Food for growing leaves,
And rain to wash past sins.

IN AND OUT OF THE UNIVERSE

Her Suns And Their Daughters: DOTUS by D.C.Thomas

I

Crescent moons are lining up
Above horizon lines,
Knots of stars are lightening up
Over time.
With stories entangled in their crossing paths,
Some turning off, some burning bright,
Waning moons are growing round,
Fiery stars are birthing dust.
Colors are framed in constellations,
Your voice in nature's orchestration
Of thinking up a sheet of music,
For my years, my mind, my confusion...
Clusters of thoughts,
Spinning around,
Across time,
Into the Universe vast.
I'm a burning star,
Orbiting your core,
Learning life's pleasantries
Can turn into treasuries,
But my soul can't just feast on them,
When it needs to know the ways of Hell,
To put balance in its parts,
To build trust in our realm.

II

Dear Universe,
Come down to me,
From wherever you are,
From beyond the skies,
From beyond the Sun,
From inside the Moon,
Come down to me
And meet me soon.
Come down to me and
I will love you,
And you will love me more,
Then I'll adore you,
And more so on...
Come down to me
And tell me stories,
Come down to me
And sing me songs.
Come down and bury these
bodies,
Mourn your children,
And let me bear some,
Once more...
Come down to me,
Don't be afraid!
I beg of you,
Come soon.

III

I dreamed of touching the Milky Way…

IV

If the Universe had chambers,
If we're to meet our makers,
We'd instigate new sets of rules,
We'd bend in space and cease be fools.

V

The Sun's love…
It casts its light
And breathes life into nothingness.
Stars do that to darkness.

VI

I dreamt of Orion's Belt at midday.

VII

The Daughters
They give birth to stones unturned,
And still lives of stories mourned,
In the ages meant to be,
They're the Daughters of the Universe Seen.

VIII

The comet shall pass,
Once circling the Sun's
Burning mass,
It'll be back
To the Universe black,
Where stars are not,
And planets bask in the dark.

IX

The farther her thoughts travel,
A new star is born,
Lives unraveled by light,
Divine gift to sight,
Humans left behind,
So others would join the tribe
Of this cosmic web
Expanding life.

X

Another orbit 'round this star,
Another year for the souls to soar,
Into the evening skies,
Filled with webs of suns
And comets breeding scars
Through darkness,
Building paths
With rocks and cosmic ice.

XI

The Sisters awake, raising their
heads
In splendid glory, mending the
Dead Suns turned to dust, amidst
the
Blurry clouds of spirals past,
Mending beasts,
the Universe
Called them, particles falling
And soaring in dense
Lines, in orbits,
Floating rings into darkness,
'til the next day's Sun rises.

XII

I wrote to her:
Who are you, bedeviling woman?
Wearing the Moon in your hair,
Stars cradling on your head?

XIII

You are the darkness in the light,
A nebula cradling stars.

XIV

Universal Promises:
We can hold the Moon in our hands,
We can live a thousand years.

XV

There's cosmic dust on your eyelashes,
Paint drying on your brushes.

XVI

I'm listening to supernovas;
Now, I want to hear your voice.

XVII

I see worlds that want to stay
hidden,
Little creatures
Who just want to listen.

XVIII

Counting the stars,
Fewer than thoughts.

XIX

We yearn for a place among the stars,
And we do nothing to outshine them.

XX

The same routine
Fills the daylight
In between
Hours of the night,
I scream,
It's dark,
I grasp a beam
With no Suns in,
This blanket of cosmic dust
Has no one here to trust.

XXI

Time doesn't exist in this room,
It doesn't even dare to know
more,
Never mention, sneak in,
We can be immortals,
Breathing in the air trapped here,
Read by the light of stars -
Make no compromise,
We'd cede the earthly things,
We'd depart from them,
Forsake mediocrity,
We'd build and build -
On the ashes of what used to be.

XXII

A Leonid meteor
Has split the November skies,
I wrote a fiery diary
Of nocturnal wishes
In the Northern Hemisphere.
Only a child had the courage
To tell me how he feels,
By the time his words will reach
me,
He shall be a man,
And I'll be grown,
Many wishes later,
Our souls we'll be reborn.

XXIII

Blueprint Monoliths

You and I - we can go back,
Erect monoliths
For today,
And paint them with inks
That we made.
You and I
Can circle the hills
Of ancient isles,
Whilst singing hymns.
You and I
Shall hold hands
Throughout the time
That shaped these lands.
Together,
We shall bring
Today
To the lands
Of yesterday.

XXIV

The rays of this neutron star
Are drawing me in,
Make it rain
With tears
In this vacuum -
Darkened by misfortune.

XXV

Orion,
Bow with your bow before me,
I lay my life at your feet,
Orion,
I travelled eons,
Amongst the stars,
I vanquished fears
To lie down in your arms.

XXVI

The red in the sky
Has faded away,
You can no longer hear
The whistles, the winds,
Nor the cliques of boys
Living here.
This ground has seen planets collide
In its vicinity,
Its cosmical path
Is changing,
Like the flickering lights of stars -
From yellows to reds -
And the neutrons'
Blues engulfing life.

XXVII

The games I play,
Life,
Are bringing stardust in -
To stay -
These games revive
The light of Sun,
They melt the snows of May
In Montana,
The ice in Siberia...
These games,
Life,
I play them better alive,
With you within;
Life, stay!
Let me play.

XXVIII

The light smitten flowers -
The ones that bloom at night -
Feed their petals on mystic powers,
They stay out of human sight.
The Fates have them in Their crowns,
Around Their mighty heads,
Holding locks of golden hairs
In place.
Their pollen falls on barren shoulders,
Blushed, warm, round,
Dewy skins under the Suns,
The Fates travel
Through the dark,
They carry the light
Harvested by petals under moons,
And stars
Of the arc.

XXIX

The only sphere I own
Possesses only curiosity -
I haven't yet fully studied its vague
anatomy,
But I look at it and I protect it - just as I
do with myself, in the mirror,
Daily,
The image is clearer if cleaner -
The glass surface bluer, truer...
In my heart, this sphere
Has no defense mechanism,
It only knows hunger,
Relentlessly, on this Earth -
This marble,
This celestial body -
People would fight for you,
Like I would,
My spiritual neighbor -
Million of light years away,
I hope my curiosity reaches you
Before my bones.
If I ever get born,
I pray my mortality
Overcomes the struggles
They and I face,
Daily.
I wish in this mirror
For us to meet and be -
Even halfway.

Her Suns And Their Daughters: DOTUS by D.C.Thomas

AT SEA

From Free Flowing Rivers…

Her Suns And Their Daughters: DOTUS by D.C.Thomas

I

The Albacore Woman

Her hands are gutting
The dead albacore,
Hands bare and scarred,
Made of flesh and bones;
The rusty vessel crosses
Murky seas,
Carrying rotting nets
Filled with fish,
And patched waders
She'd change at ease.
Her diary holds stories
'bout the waves,
Nautical miles,
Sea faring tales,
Her skin only,
Her sunburnt skin,
Ruined, ragged by the wind,
Through fishin', sleepin',

-

And in between,
Has been looted of her youth,
In spite of which,
She still feels the absolutes -
The truth she speaks with her mouth,
The love she feels with an aging heart,
The cosmic yearning of her mind,
They all bring the sleepless nights,
To this woman who ventures
Through ruffled seas
And endless thoughts.

II

The cold,
The ocean,
The depth,
The strength
Bear her head
On the shoulders carrying dread,
In the mind above their might,
Stars adorn the head - playing dead,
Closed eyes, the mind's gates,
Shed tears, they forget,
The body is hollow -
an ancient tree,
With dead bark and vanished leaves,
Scarlet freckles it reveals,
The wind banished masks she needs,
To place her steps and glide on seas.

III

The water carries sounds from deep
Reefs, sea creatures which they keep
Beyond coral branches, spirits seem
To gather life and further swim,
To hide their secrets,
Hide their deeds
Committed in our world -
Where we live, sleep and eat,
Wondering of their return
From deep within.

IV

In the eerie years which passed,
O'er the ocean's waters' blast
That drowns the sandy shores
Of barren lands,
She wails,
She sails,
When waves are calm,
At last,
She bathes,
In the sea foams
And the light Sun casts
Over mournful eyes -
Tearing o'er her past.

V

The cold,
The ocean,
The depth,
The strength...

VI

The blue hair of the Siren
Changed to waters -
All to gather
Strong men, lured to the sea,
And virgin boys
To send to sleep.
Later, the latter,
Would change into ghosts,
To praise the siren's life,
And teach her songs.

VII

The Sun rests in your eyes,
Sea waves crashing on your skin.

VIII

Ocean,
You break me,
You break my shelter,
You break my refuge,
Poseidon,
You take me,
You take my ether,
You take my breathe away with
urge...
You,
Titan,
You take me whole,
The asylum has my mind,
The sky, my eyes.
You,
Leviathan,
Have my soul.

IX

She drowned the ocean in blue inks,
Stolen from the stores across the world,
The neutron star can't evaporate the waters
Of these lands,
It's a new quarter,
With no moons, no clouds,
The haze is lingering, it shrouds -
Tree limbs hiding spiders,
Covered by the moss,
The dew in the morning
That no longer lasts,
The pigments are soaking the hem
Of this dress,
Stained again.

THE ETHER

Her Suns And Their Daughters: DOTUS by D.C.Thomas

I

There's a bee that never stops,
She flies, she whirls, she spins
Above the full of pollen plants,
In her garden full of ants
That gather, work to store
Food for the winter's coming war.

II

Drink this water,
Breathe this air,
Live this life,
And more awaits.

III

Being of light
That travels by flight
Spread thy wings, give me your
lips,
To listen, to kiss
What they pour
In my ear, in my soul,
The love and the words,
The power to soar
Alongside you,
Far away,
Right away.

IV

A ceiling holds the light,
Like the darkness bearing stars high,
To cast rays on peers alive,
And help women reunite.

V

In one way or another,
On cold days
Spent on ladders,
Made of dreams that torment,
Her hopes remain unbroken.

VI

Did you know that in the spring,
Flower blossoms are a thing?

VII

The Descent of Humans

In my absence from the sky,
I grew legs and stopped to fly,
Walked the ground,
Marched through mud
To catch the Sun,
Before it's swallowed
By a cloud.
Flattering wings,
They please the wind
Seething lands of flowers,
Burying seeds of time
In hours
Spent by timers tinned.
In the sudden moves of
clouds,
Shifts in the reddish sky,
A mournful face
Is warning rains -
Let the soul cry.

VIII

In the Highlands

Her Suns break the clouds
Made of lead,
The wind steers the sounds
Of the river
Crossing lands
Of dry grass,
Hiding lads
Watching girls
Washing plaids.
The blue in her sea of eyes
Brings the clouds
Above the grass,
In the meadow
She'll pass
Through the river banks
That bound the corners of these
lands.

IX

Nosy Noises

What is that dripping noise?
That rumble?
Never stopping…always sounding!
It comes from nowhere, then from
everywhere,
Straight to my ear. My ear!
Never-ending sounding!
Crumbling deep within,
It continues, it pours, it sounds,
In seconds of time, in hours, it spears!
Down the pipe, along the house, from
the roof,
Through the gutters, pouring, pouring,
Dripping, gathering in puddles,
Water drops, raindrops, teardrops.
A fairy crying? A cloud condensing?
A girl watering flowers?
Eh! It does not matter.
I am home.

X

The Envies collect in buckets of snow,
Frozen waters dancing in thaw,
In ponds flowing to rivers,
And forming shallow mirrors.

XI

You shattered the divine ether,
You've stolen its form and shape,
You are mimicking its spirituality
And indoctrinated all of my peers,
You stole their freedom, their bliss,
You shattered my earthly atoms,
So you'd govern the forces within.
I become invisible,
The Unseen,
You repudiated me
To a changeless life,
We won't let you obscure our hope,
We will gather in stronger numbers,
To fight you,
To prevail, to rise,
We shall build new cultures,
Again.

XII

I am the Colorado River
streaming through a torrid country,
The burnt land barely carries its people.
I am alone under the Sun,
I become a bird -
Rising to meet the turquoise sky,
You're afraid to look at me,
You fear you'll burn your eyes,
My plumage is fading,
My wings are melting,
You're aging in this labyrinth,
Let us meet,
I'd fall for you,
Let the heavens take these wings,
Let the Sun take my flight,
Keep your eyes,
Give me your heart.

THE FORESTS

Her Suns And Their Daughters: DOTUS by D.C.Thomas

I

In towns on hills,
Where forests change their leaves,
Jacks lit the porches,
And the wind has many voices.

II

There are spirits in the leaves,
They eat, they sleep,
They pour music in your ears,
They turn and rise in windy air,
They let you know of their
despair.

III

One grounded leaf
Marks an Earth in grief,
Trees standing tall,
The spine of Earth at war.

IV

In the forests, up the hill,
There's an ancient cosmic mill
Grinding earthly rocks at dawn,
Swarming dust under the Sun,
For the night to mold in stars.

V

A Tree's Cries

You may burn me, lady,
The wind will scatter my
ashes.
I pray -
This air
Won't start at your will,
Like the fire started
By your hands -
A sin,
Carried out by your kin.

VI

In the trees, at dusk,
Margins of life -
Collecting dust
Made by serpentine roads
Seen through the forests'
Leaves -
All red and gold.

VII

On the road,
On the asphalt cold
Through the forest's hold,
Trails lead to the cove
That opens up the world.

VIII

The beasts keep her awake
In shallow water,
A lake,
In the mid' of a forest -
Branches draining rain,
The beasts turn their prowling eyes
Into ghostly beads of light,
When the sleep commands her
Head, to close eyes and dream of might.

IX

Poplar trees write songs
Into this woman's heart,
She's resting by the roots,
Listening to dreams induced.

X

Those fairy lands,
Harbored by the green forests of the
Carpathian Mountains.

XI

The Passing

The waters have swallowed him,
His youth has passed into another world,
Where people don't get old,
And their daughters' worth
Is weighed in gold.

Onto the scales of his two-handed fate,
In balance, spirits rest, they wait,
On one side, the volcano is alive,
On the other, the ice is thawing into life.

Another weed is striving to grow
In this heart, about to row
To the underworld.
Universe enters dialogue,
Trading him promises in exchange for soul.
Charon saw the deed, a mischief –
It seemed to him,
For the Universe to interfere
In the passing of a low-born kid,
From a country without wit.

-

He was hidden, you see,
By his mother set free,
Taken from ruthless father's grasp
And placed into the village's safer clasp.

Charon didn't leave,
He felt nothing,
He was bound to retrieve
This boy by the shore,
And let the weed be gone.
In a time's split second –
In between,
And a decade in the world of men,
The weed spread its leaves
Around the boy, the Universe
Became a forest –
Charon's curse.

XII

The blue jays built a nest
Out of the hair I cut earlier,
Today, the tree is heavier
With burdens
And winged lives,
They lay
Their yolks and whites in gardens,
They lay their rest
And wishes,
Eggs -
Transient specks.

XIII

I seek fluttering wings,
Dried matter, colorful,
Pigmented,
Scattered,
The wind spins them,
The broken wings have gathered,
By chance,
Stuck in the gutter.

STORIES OF THE FLESH

Her Suns And Their Daughters: DOTUS by D.C.Thomas

I

I want to live in this field with you.
Loving you,
Wanting you,
Having you,
Becoming you,
Leaving you.

II

Her little mouth rests on the edge
Of a glass filled with honey,
Raw and golden,
Light and runny,
Sweet and warm
Like the boys she's yearning
During mornings ripe with light,
And soaking thighs in virgin might.

III

He was basking his mouth
In my orgasmic breath,
Tense lips and engorged lungs,
Gasping for air,
The one that left me,
Left my inside,
He did not want another kind.

IV

Lonely girls don't ask for attention,
They don't beg, they don't need,
They lust, they take,
With the greatest discretion,
No limelight to warm their path
Of destruction,
No noise to shelter
Their frustration,
Lonely girls don't ask for attention,
They're quiet with their intentions,
They walk through halls of mirrors
With no reflection,
Walk the walk
With no detection.
Lonely girls don't ask for love,
They take it, in cold blood,
To warm their veins,
And calm their pains.

V

Coal dusted lashes
Free the tears that paint the skin
Of a girl wearing tweed,
She removes them with a stroke,
Delicate fingers, heart of oak.

VI

Her wedding ring fades away,
Like a bird's, in soil, decay,
Memories of wedded days remain,
In the life of a woman's brain.

VII

Left corner of a maiden's mouth,
Eyelash underneath the eye,
A lock of hair slithers on her neck,
I lavish in a cloud of thoughts.

VIII

Maevian Biology

I'm guarded in this tower
By two hideous women,
One has my eyes,
And the other has my mouth;
I don't live in your world,
Where people wear so many masks
They can remove
Whenever they want,
By choice.
I can't remove my eyes,
I can't remove my mouth,
They feed from my soul,
Just like my heart,
They all live on my blood,
In a sickening chant.

IX

By the pillow
Filled with feathers -
Plucked yesterday,
His veins spill the blood
Of the life
She gave away.

X

Courageous Selena

My heart is not too little -
She said,
As she walked around,
With her heart and lungs exposed,
With her mind outspoken,
Loud and utter
Courage,
Rings of stars
Enlighten her,
A vessel carrying life
And strength confined,
In her eyes so bright,
A Selena in the night,
Like a Sun in the sky,
Nocturnal,
Asleep at noon,
A star in children's sight,
Outside the reach of hand,
98.6 degrees
Fahrenheit.

XI

I'm bearing in mind,
That he's another kind
Of human being.
He remains within sight,
Yet distant,
Gathering meaning
Of my wait and hesitation,
Grasping for air,
Avoid temptation,
Falling through space and
time.
Just light -
A bird in flight -
Losing wings and height,
Touching ground,
My mind he's found,
My body had,
Distraction passed,
We're touching,
He's inside.

XII

The Vessel of Life

The glasses are broken
In front of her, she smashed them with anger -
Once they were near
The trembling hands,
Now dripping blood and exhaustion,
Sipping fear from shards of glass,
This happened in the grass,
In the yard
Behind her house,
After people left,
Leaving her body outside
In the cold and wet
Air of the rain,
Putting out the flames
Of candles lit
By the same hands
That cooked the meat
For this feast -
Meant to forget that
She's carrying the child
Of a man
Already wed.

XIII

She crawls at night,
Wearing stockings
high
Her thighs,
And gently
Breathing,
Whispering,
Leaving out a sigh…

XIV

I see the wilderness in her,
The raw stream of blood,
Its unaltered course
Rushing to her cheekbones.

XV

You draw lines and circles,
I outline your spirit, your eyes,
Beautiful puzzles.
I see life in your wrists.
Have the wine,
Have me.

XVI

Tell her everything.
Pour your agony into her sweet mouth.

XVII

Feed me secrets,
Fruits I can't refuse.

XVIII

Apples cut in wedges,
Blossoms made of fruits,
And I can't eat.

Don't give me apples for my
hunger,
Nor smiles for my anger,
I don't need ice for my fever,
Nor a blanket for my shiver,
I need a kiss to quench my thirst,
And a voice to tame my lust.

XIX

My flower's pollen
Is stolen
By the wind,
It muddles with dust,
It swirls, downhill -
I miss my mother,
I miss the kiln,
The honey pots
And childish screams.
My childhood's gone,
I wish to yell - Hold on!
Instead I cry,
I summon tears,
I drown my eyes,
Birth an ocean
With waves high
To meet the sky.
It carries the petals left behind,
To my innocence,
I say goodbye.

XX

Her dress lost the thread
Holding stitches
Under the breast,
With dread -
She remained still,
No breath was taken in,
No gasp of air until
He brought his coat to her,
To shy away the eyes that hover
Upon the skin -
Through the opening of fabric seen.

XXI

One of the best endured tests
You have submitted me to
During this life trial,
Was the loss of children -
I would never have.
The air they grasped for before they had lungs,
I don't recall ever having the power to stop
your will,
But if I even had a fraction of it,
I'd use it to relinquish my breath
And give it to them.

XXII

I don't feel locked in this cage
As long as I hold the key.
The land seems uncertain to me
Outside the bars I call
The walls of my home.
The trees are sheltering fear,
The tall grass -
Predators waiting to claw the
weak,
I remain here.
 I look out and I see
You sharpening your claws,
My dear, don't forget your teeth.

XXIII

There's no life in this womb,
But death and blood,
Hairs are filling the hood
– of the coat –
Where I once stood,
Scissors in my hands
Cut the length of splitting ends
Of beauty on my head,
Bright as honey in the light,
Now, it falls aside,

Roots aging,
Leaving a shorter hair
For a woman misbehaving.

XXIV

Look at me, from that bed,
Remember what we did?
I removed the clothes,
While you did everything
To make me gasp for sweeter air,
To boldly dive into despair,
And wish for tender kisses on the said
Aging body wearing a crown of hair,
Clean, braided,
Filled with dreams - flying, sailing,
By the wind being carried,
Same air flattering the curtain,
I'm not afraid
Anymore,
I see you in the mirror…
I see the past on the floor,
I see myself searching for the
door.

XXV

In the cove,
In this shallow place, this macabre space,
Under this willow bending its children to
sleep,
With help from the wind,
Breezing in…
I wait for the shy beast,
I wait for the priest,
I wait for my blood to flood the wrist,
The left wrist I feel no more,
The wrist he kissed, and bore
The absence of the man who slumbers
In this cove.
I wait to say the words,
To cast the dark onto others, the world,
To bring him back,
Restore the life in my arm,
Then bury my voice into the ground.
The houses nearby cast no light,
The people sleep,
I hear the rats
Fleeing, the sound of water that'll come.
The wind is cooler, it stirs the earth,
The children are asleep,
I no longer sing.

XXVI

The Titans are awake,
Risen from the lake -
Drawn in this valley, by muddy
Waters, rain washing off terrains,
And sacrament ailing pains;
The blood is flooding also,
The heart is drying in my torso,
No more drumming, but red rivers
Are rushing towards the fingers,
My red life hinders,
The wrist is throbbing,
I drop the scissors.

XXVII

He's woken,
The blue ribbon unfolds
From my wrist,
His eyes are wondering,
His stature - a statue,
A craggy human body in my view,
His dormant lips roused,
Parched rosy skin,

Beloved bodied soul,
Not aware of where he's been.

XXVIII

I hear the ballads in my blood,
And I try to sing along,
I speak to women living
within,
Who dwelt in the past,
Before my skin.

XXIX

This flesh is made of women
Who aren't me,
Of men
Who know me too well,
And floorboards
Sealing the Hell.

XXX

Seven years
He spent
In this plains.
Seven years have
been
Since he played
The last game,
With cheats and less
Desire to forgive
The mistake he
made.

XXXI

The man who kisses a woman's thighs,
Is the man who makes her rise,
She sees the Sun from afar,
Then she touches the said Star.

XXXII

I'm alright
Here,
In the towers
Of my mind.
Banner-men run through dark corridors,
Blind
Spirits hide in whispered songs.
Sublime.
Every year -
Another brick,
Every day
Breeds decay,
It mounts the walls,
The stairs - spines of towering halls -
You don't seem so small to me,
Nor the world at my feet,
I only know about the distance -
The ether in between,
The space bending,
Like the wires in my knees .
You and I,
We could build bridges
Or meet in the fields,
Remain there,
Adore each other's lips,
All the flesh,
And the wits.

XXXIII

The ink has dried ,
You can turn over the card.
The water is running,
It's filling the tub,
The milk is warming
Under the Sun.
There are clean towels on the bed,
I can bring them to you, instead
I'd prefer you walk there,
In your soaked dress
Across the room,
Let the water fall,
Let me adore
The whole being of you.
Your rare smirk and pounding heart,
I want to stare
At the lines - so stark -
Without peer,
You,
The fast pace of my core,
Dear, girl,
The life you have brought!

XXXIV

The bruises in my womb,
I left them in the pool,
I'd shed everything
To forget that world .
I renew myself
In the falling snow,
My feet are cold,
I left the door open,
The steam is leaving the pool house,
Before my eyes - I see an ocean,
My new heart,
My healthy chalice overflows
With honeysuckle nectar,
And timeless vows.

Her Suns And Their Daughters: DOTUS by D.C.Thomas

THE STRUGGLE WTH ALL THE FIRES

Her Suns And Their Daughters: DOTUS by D.C.Thomas

I

Minds alike gather,
En plein air they sputter
Ideas, dreams and secrets,
Fear not someone will
listen.

II

We are pawns of life, in dreams,
Queens and kings of fate, it seems -
In our earthly realm we dare to think,
But instead of reigning, we fall to sleep.

III

We're running in a place
Where only walking is allowed.

IV

Ages ago,
I looked at her
And I found no light.
We lost each other,
Walked out of sight.

V

The webs we cast
Over eyes,
They last
Longer than a day,
They outlive us,
They stay.

VI

In bottles,
Cravings liquefy,
In drafty spaces,
Shelves supply
The potions for those who trade
Their earnings,
In exchange for gain.

VII

In the darkness, this sweet taste,
Binds the minds and mouths
Of mournful fates,
And eyes erupting threats.

VIII

Pendants weighing by the neck
Of a recluse, beauty of a wreck,
Young and spirited, she failed
To please the world who dug her grave.

IX

Her pallid heart murmurs
Fears honeyed with words
She barely utters -
In hopes of standing tall.

X

Woven linen makes the bed
Where she rests her head,
Blue heart makes the man
She spends her time to wed.

XI

Foolish minds can only wonder,
What their mouths can't simply utter,
Under trees of fallen leaves,
Under arms of warmth and bliss.

XII

Under controlled fury,
And with ego starving,
She runs through the marshes,
To meet the hero,
Fighting chances.

XIII

The gaps in her stories
Are filled with lies,
And the air around her
Brings storms in July.

XIV

The stripes of this flag,
Bring the light and blood,
Spilled by marching lads
That fought under the stars.

I do not wish to move further
Through the mud
With which you
Used to murder
My dreams and deep slumber.
I do not wish to live in this
Place
Filled with hate,
But in my dreams
Sipping bliss.

Don't go gently
Into death -
Fight or say goodbye
With a cry.

XV

In no lands have I stepped before,
Like this one, in which I wore
So much shame for being a strong girl,
And speak my mind -
Of wanting more.

XVI

I met Hypatia in my dreams,
August dreams -
Born at the roots of trees
Casting shadows over eyes
And skin burned
By the Sun -
Same star that warmed her path
On this Earth -
With rocks scattered in the sand.

XVII

These lines he draws in front of me,
Describe the land of women free
Of haters,
They dine and fight together -
The time and the weather,
As there are no men to betray
The labor
Of these honest women's nature.

XVIII

The shadows rest in the garden
Now,
Underneath the palms,
It's no more Eden,
How
Did you let this happen?
You were resting here -
By the poplar tree.

XIX

I'm hanging from a tree -
Tearing myself up from this
world,
Made of wolves and sheep,
Falling into the open ground
Beneath my dangling feet,
Where the leaves kneel
Underneath the whirls of wind
That move my fragile heels.

XX

No fair deity
Would command you
To subjugate me,
A woman,
To such cruelty,
Whilst I've been blessed
To cradle life,
And give it to this world through
pain .
I'll only obey the light,
And not your hate and spite.

XXI

I don't wish to wear the clothes
You lay on the bed
For me, every morning,
I wish to step outside
And feel the zephyr
Naked if I must,
Don't make me run away,
Wherever I'd go,
I'll stay.

XXII

My companions
Carry the candles
I'm required to light,
Instead,
I walk past the fires,
Burning dreams -
Pile by pile.

XXIII

Sir,
Lower your voice!
You need not yell at me,
You need manners,
Eyes to see,
A heart to feel
My struggle, my fear,
The strength
I beseech .
Sir,
Lower your voice!
You're only making noise,
Empty of promises,
Hollow of poise .
Sir,
I'm parting from you.
You remain a ghost, sir,
Commanding nothing,
Holding no post
In this life you cherish,
In which you lie,
And like to hate the most.

XXIV

She traces her veins
With strokes of love,
And manner of grace,
As she keeps herself
In high regard, an honest place,
Where she's at home,
Her infinite mind
In movement, through time
Becomes golden and ripe,
Bearing seeds of might
And casting light,
Like Suns in the night.

XXV

We say -
Where are you going?
Your ships are sinking,
People screaming,
The whole world prays,
Your creature obeys,
You're running games,
And send hope back in flames,
I say -
You must send the creature back,
Let it wander disembodied,
I say -
Leave its soul no more pain.
We say -
Let us sojourn in a forbidden land,
Let us be free and sane,
And we'll let you play your game,
We say -
Let us no more yell your name,
We say -
Let us sing,
We'll go away,
We say -
Let us speak,
Go away,
Take our pain,
We say -
Thy pray!

XXVI

They play the music…
And we dance.
We need to stop.
We need to think.

XXVII

To an overthinker,
Gardening could be a shot at peace,
It can be a river
Of clarity and bliss.

XXVIII

Iron walls hear the screams
Of cursed men, locked in dreams
Of terror and barred gates,
In a stronghold filled with dread.
In stoned walls, green doesn't grow,
In dark waters, beasts can glow,
In eerie times, humans grow
Poorer hearts before the dawn.
We're in the same place…
And time separates us.
Do you like that?
We only have one chance…
We only have moments.

XXIX

Something about infatuation -
Precedes good manners,
And good intentions -
Something about contemplation,
Saves my sanity
And gives me pleasure
Something about salvation -
Keeps me pure,
To pay attention
To those
Who need protection.

XXX

This tempest resting here,
Chaos unraveling,
My mind is hungry for light,
The eyes might go blind -
You're that bright,
You draw me in,
The tempest consumes me,
It shall win,
I need you here with me.

XXXI

If I mother you
I'd be gone soon,
I'd say goodbye
To my current state of mind,
And welcome thy
Life,
I'd sail away
To make you stay,
My spirit would shrink
Just so you could blink,
My arms would fall
So you could soar,
If I mother you,
My eyes would fold dreams,
While you'd walk amongst the
trees.

XXXII

That painting on the wall
Makes me cry -
I grab my shawl.
It's dark and vivid,
Bringing fear into the living;
I don't want to be still like
her,
To smile forever,
Have the time as foe,
My skin has lines -
Happy signs
Of a well lived life,
Her cosmic cold blue eyes
Bring shivers to my soul,
They outshine the Sun,
Make daring thoughts to row
Through ifs and whats,
With curiosity and doubts.

XXXIII

I am afraid today.
Nobody seems to care,
Yet they expect others
To drop everything for them;
I am afraid today,
Not only for myself,
But for this Earth,
I am afraid my voice is not loud enough,
That my words are not strong enough,
I drown in self-pity
And overwhelming doubt.
I'm a mortal who wants to overcome
This human condition
In the little time I've got
Left under this Sun.

XXXIV

Many, many leaves
Have turned in just a few days,
The Sky remained the same.
Your altruism helped me bear
The scars this world
Inflicted upon me;
I rest today,
I dream
Of you, of our father,
and the children we used to be.
I dream of mother, a being who could barely
Refuse others, naïve,
Strong - while away from others.
She'd grab your arm to twist,
Your wrist to kiss,
This fake gold you've given me
Has turned, it stains
Too many memories.

XXXV

My heart unfolded
Into a severely wrinkled map,
No one can discern the feelings -
Each left a mark -
I am a moron
Trusted by many,
Because I know this land,
But I'm just a traveller,
Burdened by its own acts.
I am a woman with too much
fight,
But weaponless and empty inside.

XXXVI

Under this weeping willow,
Under stones of ancient wisdom,
She burned the beams
That made the window,
Burned the peace of her pillow.

XXXVII

Soundless landscapes change before my eyes,
A heartless widow proceeds to pass
The houseless street I walk on now,
And thoughtless traces I leave
Of a broken vow...

XXXVIII

Mother, nothing is asked of me,
I disappoint at every turn and barely
Succeed to work this human form, indeed -
I should pray harder and try to see
The world, the people,
What lies in front of me -
Instead of walking back, believe
That I can change everything.

XXXIX

She took down the ancient masks -
They were once hanging on the wall
Of her bedroom - *doorless* and by the hall -
Where she'd enter, coming home,
Bringing strangers, remain unknown.
Her face is not wholesome -
She's cast into unknown space
And forgotten times - gruesome -
Depiction of what she's now,
A past portrayal of a wooden prow;
Half the former, half the latter,
They both struggle to matter,
But no common ground is found,
'cause one of them has drowned,
Whilst other lives scattered
On this planet anchored.

XL

Sunken Titans,
Titans frighten
This lion,
Titans darken
The horizon,
The longest shadows have been cast,
The Titans have claws, they move fast
In this world orbiting the Star,
I'm not leaving, I'd fall,
I'm staying, standing,
Six foot tall,
On heels, expensive, gotten from the mall,
Some Titans wear lipstick,
Red polish on their claws,
The Titans have beauty in the man-made light,
I am dependent on these walls around,
I decide to break them down,
And expose the Titans to the Sun.

XLI

Is survival:
Lying,
Running,
Hiding?

XLII

You can hurt me
After you moved the Sun,
You may call me whatever you wish -
After you came up with a plan
To move Earth
On a better path,
Closer to Andromeda;
You may yell at me
After you filled my eyes with stars
I haven't yet looked at,
You may count my scars
If you placed a quasar in a jar,
For me to have, on the nightstand -
You may not hold my hand.

XLIII

The deities have dropped to their knees,
We, humans, killed all the bees,
Our children have no honey left,
I weep,
I want to go to sleep.
All the fires are out,
And the light they kept in town.
These beads are not mine,
They belonged to my mother,
She broke the necklace they made,
And the chains she held.
My legs won't carry me to your door,
My heart won't sow
Any love or care your way,
I wish to stay
Here, where I am plain
And I love myself,
Despite the pain.

XLIV

My skin is drinking the water
Of the river,
My ears are wearing the last
Words you said to me - their echo is filling the
space
Around me, they bend it.
All of my white shirts are at the dry cleaners,
My wrist watch can't keep up
With the passing of time, as I perceive it -
And the seconds left behind,
Like breadcrumbs.
Is it pity?
Is the Universe giving me chances?
Catching up on living?
Is it you, convincing me of not quitting?

XLV

There's a wasp
On the hanging rod
Of the fan -
It made it inside,
After the Sun was gone;
I turned the fan on,
It's cold
Again - it's dawn,
The wasp has flown.

Now,
I keep looking up,
I keep screwing up…
Where are you, Sun?

XLVI

We should hide the candlesticks,
And put away the lighter,
The fires have started
In the forest;
Don't forget the letters
We sent to each other,
Over this summer.
I'll start the car,
You need to pack,
And we'll go far
Away from here,
Before the fires reach that fir
Tree, on the hill;
If this cottage burns
I'll keep the ashes in urns,
And plant more ferns
By the fence surrounding it;
Don't be sad,
We have water,
We have tears,
Time will wash the fires,
It all fits
In the cosmic scheme of things.

XLVII

They burnt all the books,
They searched all the nooks
In her house.
The stairs collapsed
Under the fire they started -
In the atrium,
Where the walls are scarlet -
Now, they bask in flames
And soot,
She's surrounded,
Guarded,
She can't fight with shackles on,
She's watching the roof going down,
Wait awhile, she says to self,
I can make fires too.

XLVIII

I didn't want to close the door in your
face
Today, but it was the only thing
I could do
To keep you away.
I know it was without grace,
My gesture - it made me cry
Behind the wood that makes the door,
Where I stand, the floor
Is swallowing me whole .
The blizzard's almost gone,
Our hearts bear more weight -
Drowned in sorrow,
The winds will stop screaming soon,
I'll stay by the fire
Until tomorrow, at noon.

XLIX

They cut the trees in the backyard,
The flowers I planted
Mixed with the mud -
Under their heavy boots;
It rained the day before,
They drank the waters
The sky poured,
The soil is drenched;
I want them gone,
They don't belong -
In this city,
In this world,
This is my only home.

L

I am the only one
Who can see the snake wrapped around your
tongue.
I can hear the glacier's ice,
Slowly - moving into thaw,
The land, here, is barren,
No fields to sow,
But oceans and caves,
Where can we go?
For food and rest,
So we can grow?
I'll bear children and teach them
To let other humans know -
That you cursed us,
You brought the snake among,
A long time ago.

LI

The enumeration of your smiles
Would make for compelling vows.
In front of so many people -
I stand,
Here, looking at the walls
Listing memories in faded hues,
The Sun's light has sneaked through
The blinds,
Through the ages, they've been
drawn...
I see the crescent moon now,
People yawn.
Please, ask all these people to leave,
They're not stars,
Not meant to be here.
I only need your light,
Close the curtains,
Close your eyes,
We'll travel,
We'll be alright.

LII

She has thousands of mouths
In her purse,
Broken necklaces at the bottom of it,
Entangling secrets with beads,
All, under a rusting zipper.
The social needs drained her,
The formal dresses are alone
At the dry-cleaners,
She won't pick them up.
The secrets and lovers remain,
She's a mother,
Living on loans,
She changes her own tires,
She does nothing in vain,
She grows.

LIII

The silent dorms in this neighborhood
Are like garden sheds, with no room
For ghosts like me -
Wandering the streets -
All the matter's eaten by rust,
All people are devoid of trust.
We're left to breathe on a battleground,
We use no tools,
We need no food,
All is drowned,
Defiant of time.

LIV

These birds, all gather,
And circle the garden
Where the Robin lost its wings,
Chariots lost their wheels - long ago,
Now buried here,
With men mourned by widows,
Ancient years,
In these fields, plowed by daughters
Coping with grief,
The lamentation, the woe,
They haven't gone too far,
Plato, talk to me,
I am real, I am here,
I don't want to bury you in this field,
Talk to me or I will set the Robin
free.

LV

We are not in love with nature,
As we keep fighting our own:
From cavemen to social butterflies,
To birdcages during difficult times.
We are not one with nature,
Like we ask others to be -
While we keep pushing buttons
On devices and never agree
Online, where we pour our time and energy.
From these birdcages,
We make pleas and feed our narcissism,
We ask for attention and beg others
To give us the time they don't have,
And pin us higher in their lives.

"Monolith", Linocut Print by D.C.Thomas

to be continued… in PAWNS:

Poor Artists Wedding Neutron Stars

Gratitude,

D.C.Thomas

D.C.THOMAS

Copyright © 2020 D.C.Thomas

ISBN: 9798599922087

The *Her Suns And Their Daughters,
Daughters Of The Universe Seen* anthology by
D.C. Thomas has been registered with the United
States Copyright Office in 2020.

*From The Library of Congress, The United States
Copyright Records:
Registration Number/Date:
TX002190980/2020-03-31*

*Cover Art by D.C.Thomas, detail
"Simplicity Isn't Emptiness", Acrylic on paper*

Made in the USA
Columbia, SC
15 September 2023